Charlie
and
the Curious Club
Candy or Medicine?

By Erainna Winnett

Illustrated by Somnath Chatterjee

Charlie and the Curious Club
Candy or Medicine?
Text copyright © 2013 by Erainna Winnett
Illustrations copyright © 2013 by Somnath Chatterjee

Author: Erainna Winnett
Illustrator: Somnath Chatterjee

Printed in the United States of America

Summary: Charlie and his best friend discover the importance of mistaking medicine for candy.

ISBN: 0615907768
ISBN: 978-0615907765

Library of Congress Cataloging-in-Publication Data
Charlie and the Curious Club
Candy or Medicine?
Library of Congress Control Number:2013919603

www.counselingwithheart.com

To my nephew, may your light
continue to shine.

Charlie McCloud was curious by nature. Even ordinary things, like regular old apples, sent his wheels a-spinning.

"What makes some apples red, and others green? Does eating one a day really keep the doctor away?"

Charlie crunched down to the core. "Pfft!" He spit a round seed onto the table. "Hey, Mom, if I planted this, would an apple tree grow?"

Mom smiled. "Sounds like an investigation for the Curious Club."

Charlie pumped his fist. "Sure does! I'm going to call Dillin over for a special meeting." Charlie scooped up three apples from the basket and headed outside to the treehouse.

Dillin arrived minutes later and got right to work investigating. "Look at the shape of this seed!" he said.

"Neat," said Charlie. "But I haven't figured out whether or not apples are like medicine, and can really keep the doctor away. Want to help me look in this book?"

"Sure." Dillin reached to take the book from Charlie's hand when a loud thunk stopped them both.

"What was that?" asked Charlie.

The boys peered out and saw a moving truck pull in next door.

A lady with tight gray curls stepped out— and sitting on her shoulder was a parrot!

"We can investigate apples and doctors later." Charlie stated. "Right now, the Curious Club has to find out about our new neighbor and her pet parrot!"

"Yeah," exclaimed Dillin. "Why doesn't it just fly away?"

The boys ran inside to ask Mrs. McCloud if they could meet the new neighbor and learn more about her unusual pet.

"Sure," said Mrs. McCloud. "I've already met Ms. Shirley. She seems very nice."

The ding-dong of the doorbell was followed by a loud *Caw! Caw!*

"Pierre , shhh," said the gray-haired lady as she opened the front door. "Good afternoon. I'm Ms. Shirley, and this noisy guy is Pierre. Come on in!"

As Charlie entered the living room, new questions flooded his mind. There were so many things he'd never seen before! What should he investigate first?

Caw! Caw!

Pierre's squawks reminded Charlie of their mission. "Ms. Shirley, why doesn't Pierre fly away?"

Ms. Shirley reached for Pierre as she sat on the sofa. "His wing is clipped, see?"

Dillin took notes in the Curious Club journal, and made a sketch of Pierre's clipped wing. Ms. Shirley asked what Dillin was doing. Charlie explained all about the Curious Club, and that gave him an idea. "I know! Pierre can be the third member of our Club!"

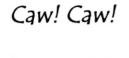

Caw! Caw!

Pierre squawked and flapped his wings. "I guess he approves!" Ms. Shirley laughed. "Would you boys like some lemonade?"

Both boys nodded and Ms. Shirley headed into the kitchen.

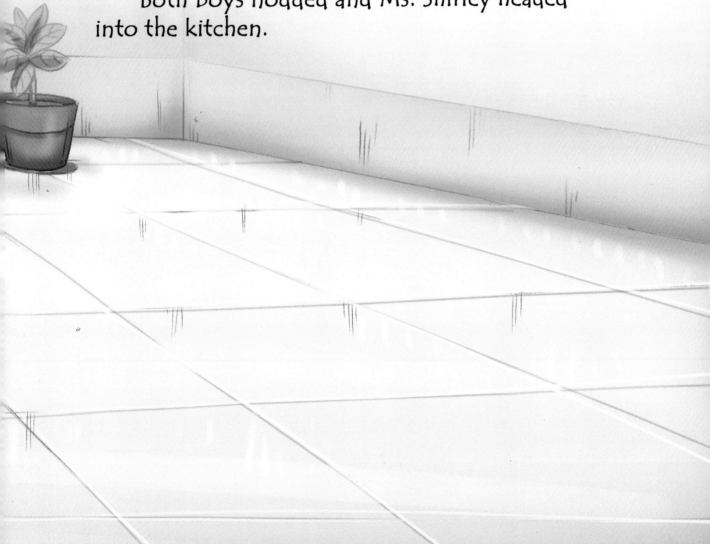

Charlie wandered around the room. "Look at all the stuff!"

Dillin picked up an odd-looking gadget.

Charlie spotted a colorful trinket on the table. "I think there's a new kind of candy over here," Charlie whispered. "Do you think the red ones are strawberry or cherry?"

"That's a strange-looking dish," Dillin added.

"What do you suppose the letters mean?"

"Sounds like an investigation for the Curious Club!" Charlie exclaimed.

Caw! Caw! Pierre hurried his way to the table.

"Why is he pecking like that?" Charlie asked.

Dillin shrugged. "Maybe it's his candy."

"Let's take some candies back to the treehouse anyway. We can taste them there."

"Did someone say candies? I love candies!" Ms. Shirley entered with a tray of lemonade, but nearly dropped it when she saw what the boys were investigating. "Oh, dear! That's not candy! That's medication in my special container. It has exactly the right amount that I need to take each day."

"So that's what the letters are for!" Dillin said.

"Pierre was trying to warn us!" Charlie added.

"Being curious is a good thing, boys. But curiosity without caution is dangerous. Do you know what happens if you take too much medicine or if you take the wrong kind?"

"Something bad?" Charlie guessed.

"Look here, in this poison safety book," said Ms. Shirley.

Charlie read out loud. "Tummy aches, vomiting, a visit to the hospital...oh no! This is something the Curious Club NEEDS to know more about right now. May we borrow this?"

"Of course," replied Ms. Shirley, "on one condition. Whatever you learn, the Curious Club will share with other children."

While they studied the poison safety book and munched on apples—they "kept the doctor away" and made a new pledge for the Curious Club.

And later, they kept their promise to share all they learned with kids like you!

Hey Parents and Teachers!
Keep your Curious Children Safe by:

1. Locking up medicines and household products, where children cannot see or reach them.

2. Store products only in their original containers.

3. Using child-resistant packaging…but remembering, NOTHING is childproof!

4. Taking medicines or poisonous products with you when you answer the door or the phone.

5. Never calling medicine candy.

6. Taking medicines when children cannot see you.

7. Teaching your children to ask a grown-up before touching, smelling, or tasting something unknown.

8. Finding opportunities such as Red Ribbon Week (second week in October) to talk with children about the dangers of mistaking medicine or household products for candy or sweet drinks!

CPSIA information can be obtained at www.ICGtesting.com
Printed in the USA
LVIW01n1639161117
556555LV00012B/143

9 7 8 0 6 1 5 9 0 7 7 6 5